That night said, "Let's

watch a scary movie. *The*

from the Swamp is

on !"

"Arf!" barked .

"Don't forget the ,"

said .

GARFIELD Picture Clue Book

MONSTER TROUBLE

Written by Scott Nickel
Illustrated by Mike Fentz and Lori Barker
Designed by Kenny Goetzinger

Garfield created by
JIM DAVIS

Scholastic Reader — Level 1

ISBN 0-439-66977-4

12 11 10 9 8 7 6 5 4 3 2 1   4 5 6 7 8 9

Printed in the U.S.A.
First printing, September 2004

SCHOLASTIC INC.
New York   Toronto   London   Auckland   Sydney
Mexico City   New Delhi   Hong Kong   Buenos Aires

It was Halloween. was

outside making the

look spooky.

He put up a , ,

rubber , and a .

ate . "I am so

not scared," said .

made three

of . 's was the

biggest.

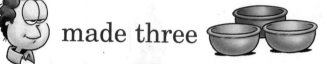, , and  sat

on the .

"Let's switch off the so it

will be extra spooky!"

said .

"This movie won't scare me,"

said .

The on growled

and waved its .

Suddenly, there was thunder and . The  shook.  and  were scared. "?" said . But  was not there. Where did he go?

 and  heard a

noise in the  . They

looked out the  . Was it

 ? No! It was a  —

just like the one on  !

 jumped.

 gulped.

"We can't let the from

the Swamp get in the ,"

 said to 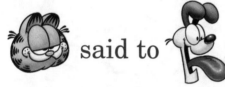.

"We have to set a trap by

the 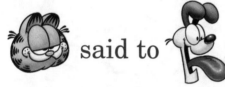."

stood on a . He

hung a on a over

the . He filled the

with .

"This will stop the !"

said .

"Arf!" barked .

The opened and the

 fell. *Splash!* The trap

worked.

"We got the !" said

.

"Arf! Arf!" barked .

It was only .

 and  pointed to

the .

"Look! The from the

Swamp!" said .

"That's not a ," said .

"It's a mask. I put it

in the by the ,

, , and .

I finally scared you, !"

"Ha!" said . "The only

thing that scares *me* is

running out of ."

Did you spot all of the picture clues in this Garfield Halloween story?

Each picture clue is on a flash card. Ask a grown-up to cut out the flash cards. Then try reading the words on the back of the cards. The pictures will be your clue.

Reading is fun with Garfield!

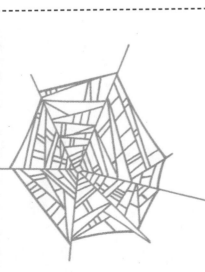

Garfield	Jon
pumpkin	Odie
bats	cobwebs

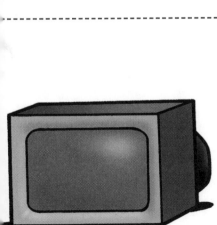

house	ghost
monster	candy
popcorn	television

couch	bowls
hands	lamp
bushes	lightning

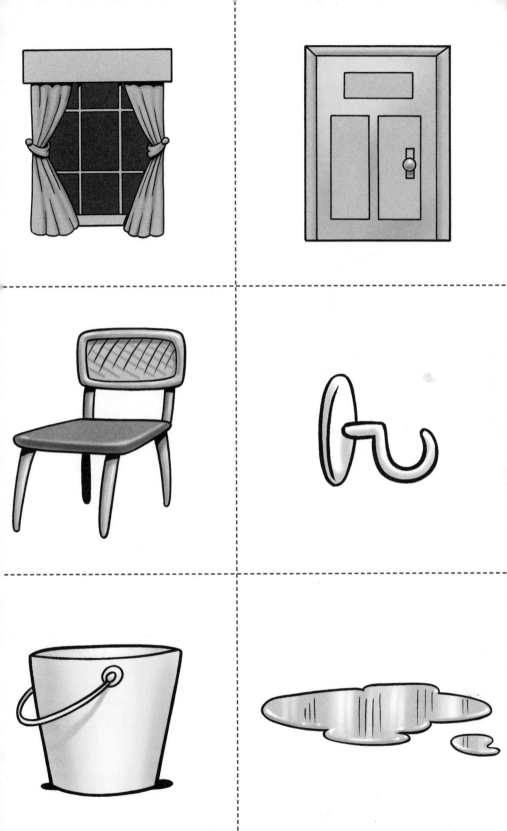

door	window
hook	chair
water	bucket